SNOW ON SNOW ON SNOW

Cheryl Chapman
paintings by Synthia Saint James

Dial Books for Young Readers New York

With thanks to Pierce Pettis

Published by Dial Books for Young Readers
A Division of Penguin Books USA Inc.
375 Hudson Street
New York, New York 10014

Designed by Amelia Lau Carling
Printed in Hong Kong
First Edition
3 5 7 9 10 8 6 4 2

Library of Congress Cataloging in Publication Data
Chapman, Cheryl.
Snow on snow on snow / Cheryl Chapman ;
pictures by Synthia Saint James.—1st ed.
p. cm.
Summary: The author uses repetitive word play
to tell the story of an African-American boy who loses
and then recovers his dog while sledding in the snow.
ISBN 0-8037-1456-4 (trade).—ISBN 0-8037-1457-2 (lib. bdg.)
[1. Snow—Fiction. 2. Dogs—Fiction. 3. Sleds—Fiction.
4. Afro-Americans—Fiction.] I. Saint James, Synthia, ill.
II. Title. PZ7.C366365Sn 1994 [E]—dc20 93-6278 CIP AC

The artwork was rendered in oil and acrylic on canvas.
It was then color-separated and reproduced in full color.

To Winslow and Casey, friends,
with love
C.C.

For Michele, Jessica, Eja, and Sade
S.S.J.

In the bleak midwinter,
    Frosty wind made moan,
Earth stood hard as iron,
    Water like a stone;
Snow had fallen, snow on snow,
    Snow on snow,
In the bleak midwinter,
    Long ago.

from "In the Bleak Midwinter"
by Christina Rossetti (1830–1894)

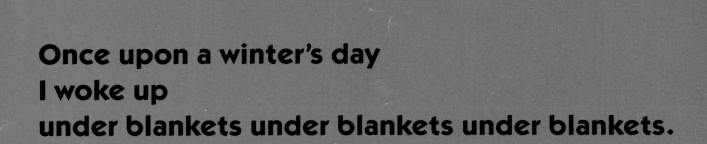

**Once upon a winter's day
I woke up
under blankets under blankets under blankets.**

At breakfast
Mama filled up my plate
with food next to food next to food.

I pulled on
clothes over clothes over clothes.

**We stepped out the door
into snow on snow on snow.**

**We climbed
up the hill up the hill up the hill
and found our friends...**

on sleds beside sleds beside sleds.

We zoomed
down down down
the slopes,

spinning out at the end.

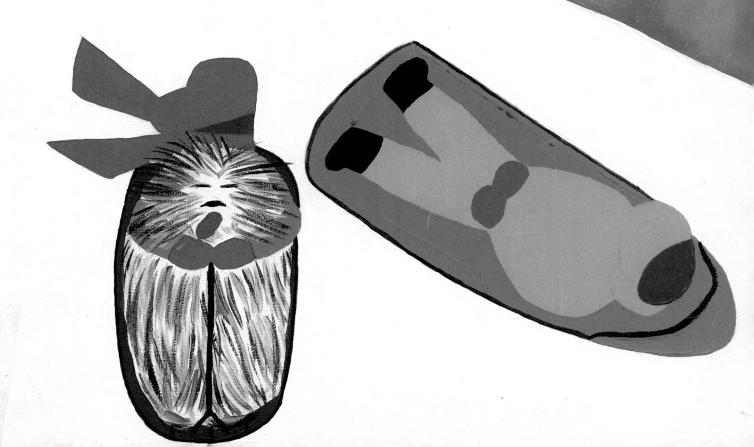

But where did Clancy go?

We looked

behind trees

behind trees

behind trees.

We searched
around bushes
around thickets
around cattails.

Clancy had disappeared
into the snow
into the wind
into the air.

**Tears on tears on tears
froze my face.**

**Below drifts below drifts below drifts of snow
there came a woof.**

**And
we all lived
happily
ever after ever after ever after.**